P9-DMC-145

ASHER AND THE CAPMAKERS
A HANUKKAH STORY

by Eric A. Kimmel
illustrated by Will Hillenbrand

Holiday House/New York

Once upon a time a charcoal maker
and his wife lived in the forest high in the
Carpathian mountains. They had seven children:
six girls and a boy named Asher. Asher loved the
forest. Its hidden paths were as familiar to him as
the cracks in the ceiling above his bed.

One Hanukkah Eve, the family began
making potato latkes. Alas! They realized
they had no eggs.

"Bring an egg from the
henhouse," Asher's mother
told him.

Asher went to the henhouse, but all the nests were empty.

"I'll borrow an egg from our neighbor," Asher said.

"No, it's too dark outside," said his mother.

"We can do without latkes for one night," his father added.

"Don't worry. I'll be back before you light the Hanukkah candles," Asher told them as he set out for their neighbor's house.

Snow began falling.
Asher pushed on, though
he could no longer see
the path. He hoped he
was going in the
right direction.

One by one the stars came out. *"I must have strayed from the path. I've never been in this part of the forest before,"* Asher thought.
Just then he heard a sharp bark.
He saw a fox caught in a snare.

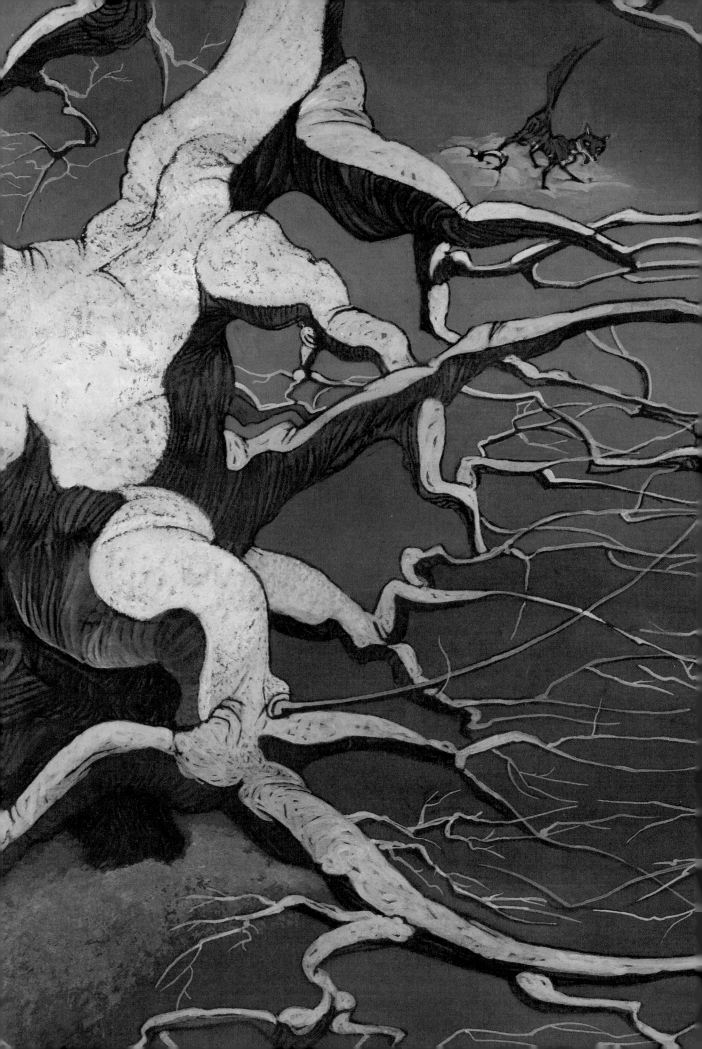

Asher released the fox. "Poor creature. Neither of us should be out tonight."

The fox ran a few paces, then stopped to look back over its shoulder. It ran a little farther, then stopped again.

"It wants me to follow," Asher realized. He hesitated at first, for he knew that evil spirits sometimes take the shape of animals. "But if I stay here, I may freeze to death. Could this be a good spirit sent to help me?" Asher decided to follow the fox.

The fox led Asher through the snow-covered forest. A light appeared in the distance. The fox raced toward it. Asher followed. The fox's tracks led to a little house with a lamp shining above the door. Asher knocked.

A tiny old woman with the bright, sparkling eyes of a fox opened the door. She wore a peculiar red cap.

"Come in. Warm yourself by the hearth," the woman said. When Asher went inside he saw two other women busily sewing caps. One wore a green cap. The other wore a blue cap. Red, blue, and green caps covered the floor. The woman in the red cap sat down and began sewing too. Hours passed.

Finally the woman in the red cap got up and spread a blanket on the floor. "Sleep here," she told Asher. The three capmakers climbed into the cupboard, taking the candle with them.

But Asher did not go to sleep. His parents had warned him about elves, fairies, and other creatures that haunt the forest by night. He was certain these women were not human beings.

The fire on the hearth burned low as the wind rattled the windowpanes. Asher lay awake, watching and listening.

Suddenly the door flew open. A troop of tiny people swept in. "It's time!" they sang. The three capmakers jumped out of the cupboard. "It's Hanukkah Eve. Where will we go?" Green Cap asked.

"Where else? To Jerusalem!" Red Cap replied. Whoosh! Before Asher's astonished eyes, she flew up the chimney.

"To Jerusalem!" the others echoed, plucking caps from the floor. The magic caps whisked them up the chimney, one after another, until all were gone and only one cap remained. Asher tried it on.

"To Jerusalem," he said, just to see what would happen.

WHOOSH! Up the chimney he went!

Asher flew through the night. He saw the lights of towns and villages far below. Then came a darkness where the air tasted of salt. Asher knew he was crossing the sea . . .

And then he was flying over Jerusalem! Here was the

Temple Mount . . . and the Western Wall . . . and King
David's Tower. Asher recognized them from the pictures
in the family bible. A large building loomed up ahead.
It was the pasha's palace. Asher swooped down the
chimney.

Thump! He landed in the fireplace. Asher found himself in a vast banquet hall. An enormous chandelier hung from the ceiling. A table set for a great feast ran the length of the hall. In the center, below the chandelier, stood a towering cake lit with candles.

"Welcome!" a thousand voices cried at once. The hall was filled with capmakers. Some were as tall as Asher. Some were as tiny as a sparrow. Each wore the same peculiar cap.

Music began to play, a wild swirling tune. The capmakers took Asher's hands, formed a circle, and began to dance. Around and around they whirled, across the floor, over the chairs, onto the table.

Chiribim! Chiribom!
Chiribim-bom-bim-bom-bim-bom!

Faster and faster.

Chiribom! Chiribim!
Chiribim-bom-bim-bom-bim-bom!

Asher and the capmakers danced around the cake,
in and out among the platters, up the wall and onto the
ceiling, circling the chandelier. Asher saw the plaster
beginning to crack. "Look out!" he yelled. But the capmakers only whirled faster.

Ay! Chirbiribiribiri-bim-bom!
Ay! Chirbiribiribiri-bim-bom!
Ay! Chirbiribiribiri-bim-bom!
Chiribim-bom-bim-bom-bom. Hey!

The ceiling collapsed. The chandelier crashed onto
the table. Cake and capmakers flew everywhere. Asher
landed in the pasha's chair, covered with cake from
head to foot. His cap fell off. It rolled under the chair.

Suddenly he heard a pounding at the door. "Open at
once!"

The capmakers leaped from the wreckage. "We're off!"
they cried. Like smoke, they flew up the chimney.
"I'm off too!" Asher cried. But nothing happened,
for he had lost his cap.

The door burst open. The pasha stormed into the room,
followed by soldiers. "It's happened again! My feast
is ruined!"

"Excellency, one of the villains is sitting
in your chair!" The soldiers pointed to Asher.

"Arrest him!" the pasha cried. Before Asher could recover his cap, the soldiers seized him and dragged him before the pasha.

"Speak, Villain!" the pasha said. "How did you get into my palace?"

Asher refused to say a word. He knew no one would believe him.

The pasha turned to his soldiers. "Take this thief to the gallows. He came to steal, so fill his pockets with gold before you hang him. That will give his neck a good stretch."

Asher stood before the gallows.

"Any last requests?" the hangman asked.

"May I borrow an egg?" Asher replied. "And if it isn't too much trouble, would you look for my cap? I lost it in the pasha's banquet hall. My mother made that cap for me. I'd like to wear it when I die."

"I will do what I can," the hangman promised. He sent his assistant back to the palace. The man returned shortly, with the egg and the cap.

Asher placed the egg in his pocket. He put the cap on his head.

"Any last words?" the hangman asked as he slipped the noose around Asher's neck.

"Yes," said Asher. "I'm off!"

WHOOSH! And off he went, leaving Jerusalem far behind.

Asher flew through the night, over forests and oceans, until he reached his home. Whoosh! The cap set him down by his door. Then it vanished. Asher saw the menorah standing in the window with the candles lit for the first night of Hanukkah. A memorial candle stood beside it. *"I wonder who died?"* he thought.

Asher knocked on the door. "Mother, I'm home.
I brought the egg. And more!"

The door opened. Asher's mother stared as if she had
seen a ghost. "Asher!" she gasped, and fainted.

"Asher has returned!" his father and sisters cried.

Only then did Asher learn the truth. It was indeed
the first night of Hanukkah, but seven years had passed
since he left to borrow the egg.

That is the story of Asher, the boy who met the capmakers. Today, if you go to a certain village high in the
Carpathian mountains, the people there will show you
one of the coins he brought back from Jerusalem. For
this is a true story.

The moon and the sun,
This tale's begun.
The cow's in the clover,
My story is over.

Author's Note

In writing this original tale, I have combined motifs of fairy lore from Ireland, England, and Eastern Europe. Like other mortals who encounter the fairy folk, Asher is whisked away on an adventure across time and space. Capmakers, or *kapelyushniki*, are Jewish fairies. For some reason, they are always described as busily making hats. King David's Tower, the Western Wall, and the Temple Mount where the Mosque of Omar stands are all landmarks in Jerusalem. *Latkes* or potato pancakes are part of the tradition of Hanukkah, the Festival of Lights. Latkes are made from onions, salt, meal, pepper, and eggs. A *pasha* is a Turkish official. The Ottoman Turks ruled Jerusalem and the Holy Land for four hundred years, from 1517 to 1917. Finally, the song "Chiribim! Chiribom!" is a rollicking Yiddish folk song.

ERIC A. KIMMEL
January 15, 1993

To Will
E.A.K.

For Katy & Carly,
with special thanks to Irene Frieman
W.H.

Text copyright © 1992 by Eric A. Kimmel
Illustrations copyright © 1993 by Will Hillenbrand
All rights reserved
Printed in the United States of America
First Edition

This story first appeared in *Cricket, The Magazine for Children*

Library of Congress Cataloging-in-Publication Data
Kimmel, Eric A.
Asher and the capmakers : a Hanukkah story / by Eric A. Kimmel ; illustrated by Will Hillenbrand. — 1st ed.
p. : ill. ; cm.
Summary: On his way to get an egg for his mother the night before Hanukkah, a young boy encounters
a group of mischievous fairies who take him on an adventure to Jerusalem.
ISBN 0-8234-1031-5
[1. Fairy tales.   2. Jews—Fiction.   3. Jerusalem—Fiction.]   I. Hillenbrand, Will, ill.   II. Title.
PZ8.K527As   1993   92-37978   CIP   AC
[E]—dc20

10/93

GAYLORD
S